P9-DDQ-936

For Mom, with love from Kristina

Other Schiffer Books By The Author:
The Fish Tank, 978-0-7643-3706-2, $16.99
The Turtle Tank, 978-0-7643-3843-4, $16.99

Library of Congress Control Number: 2011927310

Type set in Tabby/Edwardian Script

ISBN: 978-0-7643-3842-7
Printed in China

Schiffer Books are available at special discounts for bulk purchases for sales promotions or premiums. Special editions, including personalized covers, corporate imprints, and excerpts can be created in large quantities for special needs. For more information, contact the publisher:

Published by Schiffer Publishing Ltd.
4880 Lower Valley Road
Atglen, PA 19310
Phone: (610) 593-1777; Fax: (610) 593-2002
E-mail: Info@schifferbooks.com

For the largest selection of fine reference books on this and related subjects, please visit our website at www.schifferbooks.com
We are always looking for people to write books on new and related subjects. If you have an idea for a book please contact us at the above address.

This book may be purchased from the publisher.
Include $5.00 for shipping.
Please try your bookstore first.
You may write for a free catalog.

In Europe, Schiffer books are distributed by
Bushwood Books
6 Marksbury Ave.
Kew Gardens
Surrey TW9 4JF England
Phone: 44 (0) 20 8392 8585; Fax: 44 (0) 20 8392 9876
E-mail: info@bushwoodbooks.co.uk
Website: www.bushwoodbooks.co.uk

The Rat Tank

Kristina Henry

Illustration by Laura Ambler and Amanda Brown

4880 Lower Valley Road Atglen, Pennsylvania 19310

Brown rat spins round and
Round. Legs move on wheel while his
Friend chews and nibbles.

Tank is big and clear,
With lots of tunnels. The rats
Explore surroundings.

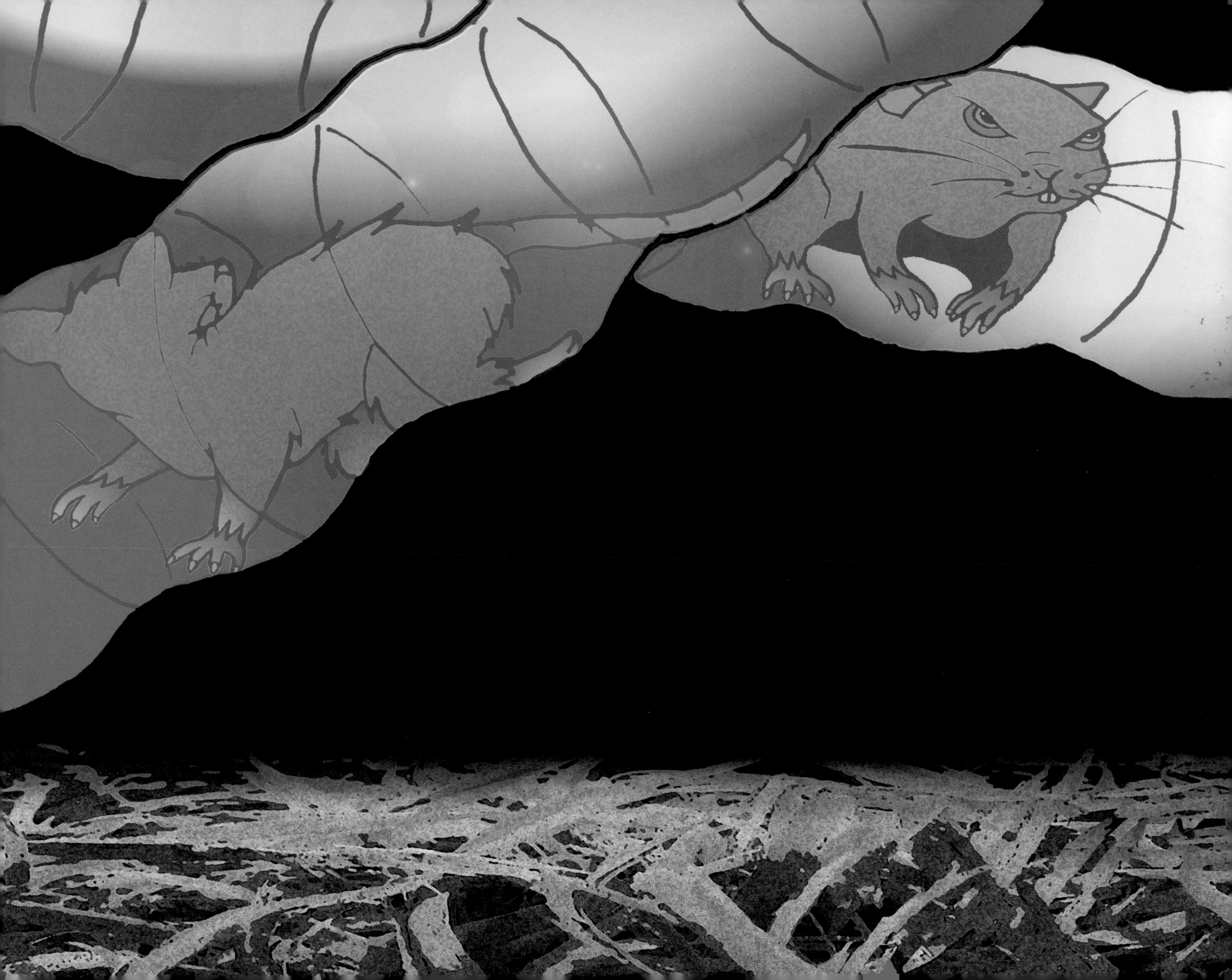

Soft floor smells of wood.
With lots of water and food,
The rat tank is nice.

No hide and seek games.
Rats stay apart. Live alone.
Nighttime comes. They sleep.

Morning brings new food
And drink. Gray rat nibbles, gnaws,
And chews. Brown rat runs.

New day, same routine.
Except gray rat climbs through tube.
Oh no! He is stuck!

Brown rat runs. Wheel turns.
Gray rat huffs. He sighs, pushes.
Listens as wheel turns.

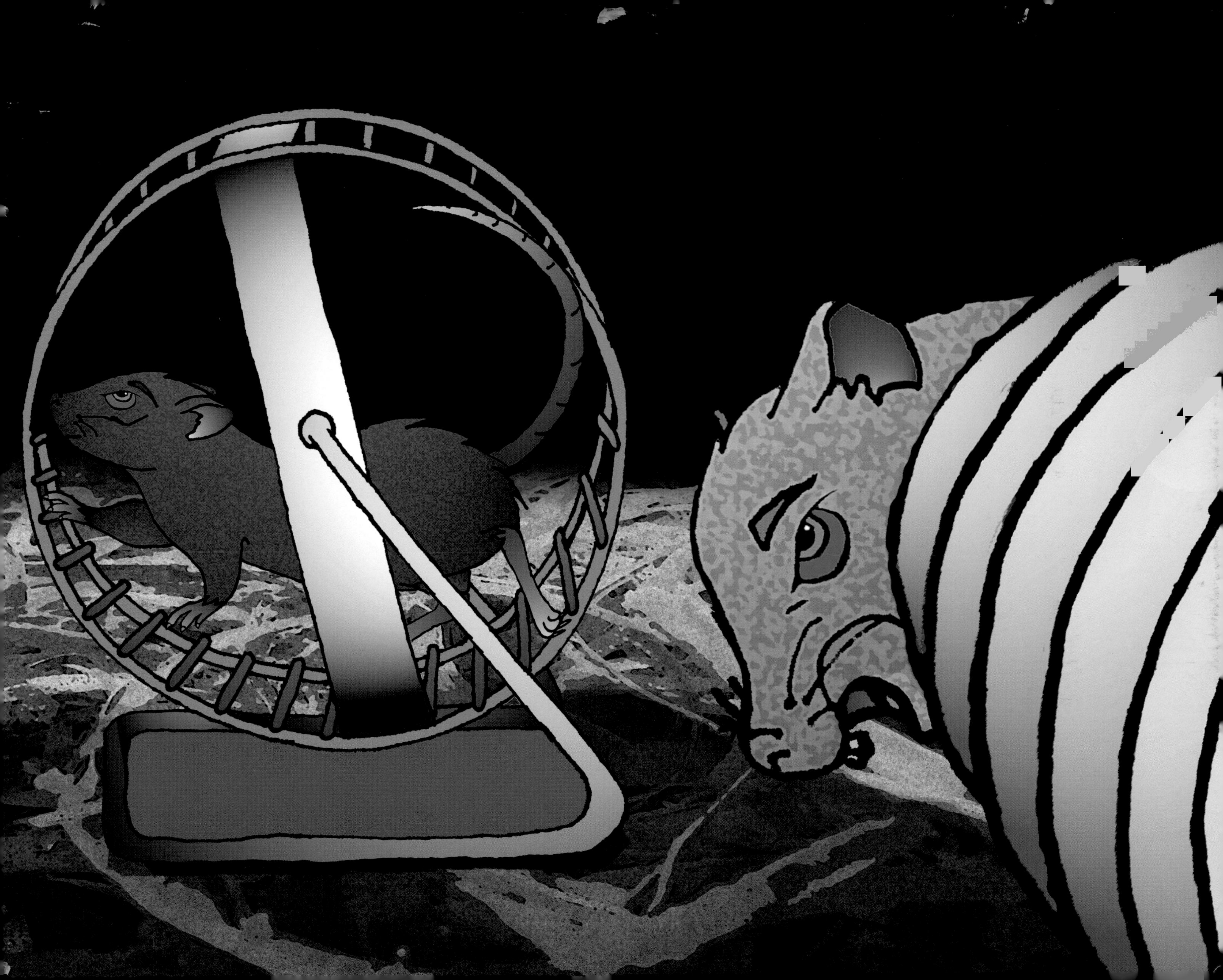

Gray rat shrieks! Brown rat
Can't hear. Wheel makes too much noise.
Gray rat shrieks once more.

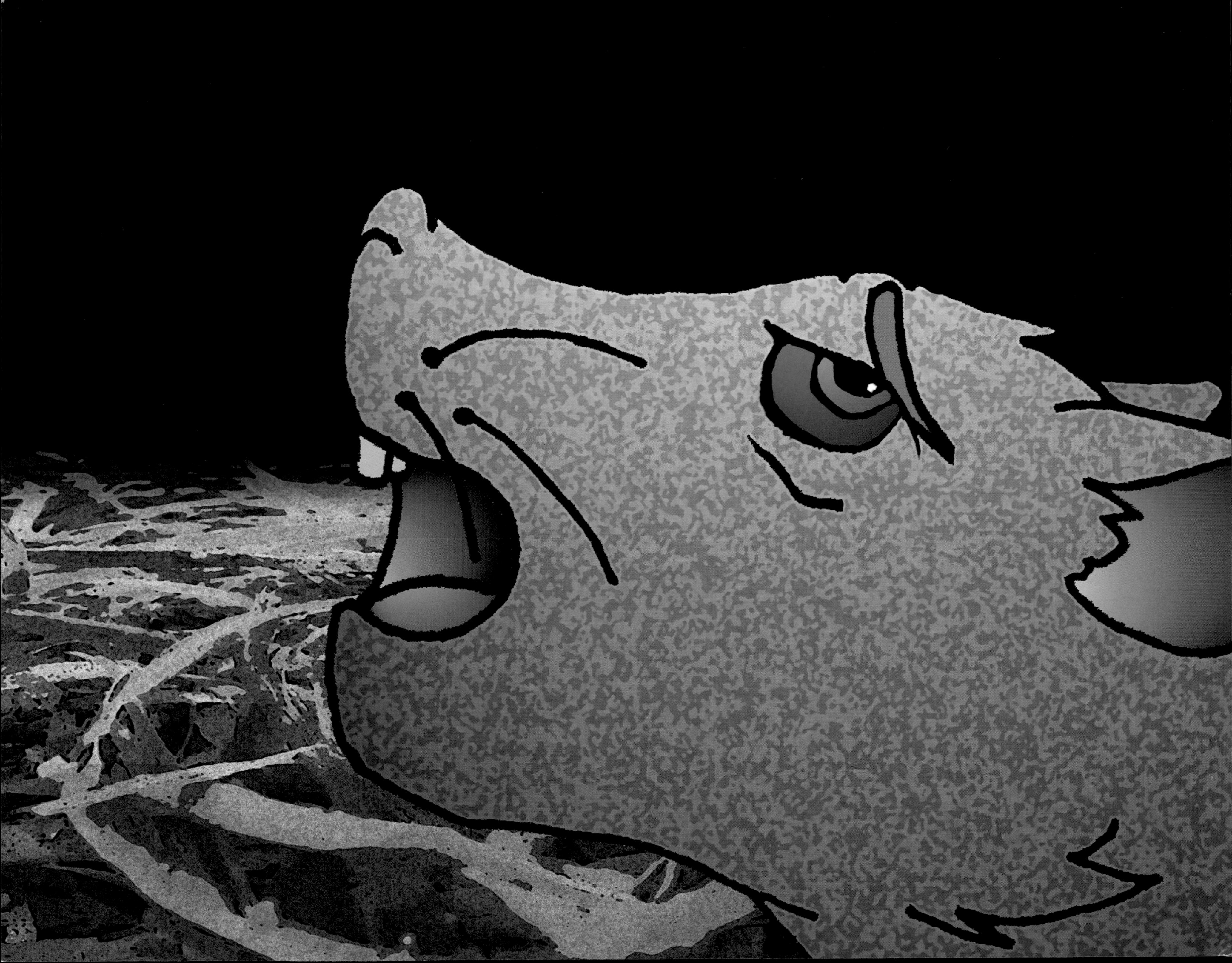

Brown rat stops. Listens.
His whiskers twitch. His ears move.
Another loud shriek.

Brown rat climbs tunnel.
He sees feet and a pink tail.
He stops, sniffs. He thinks.

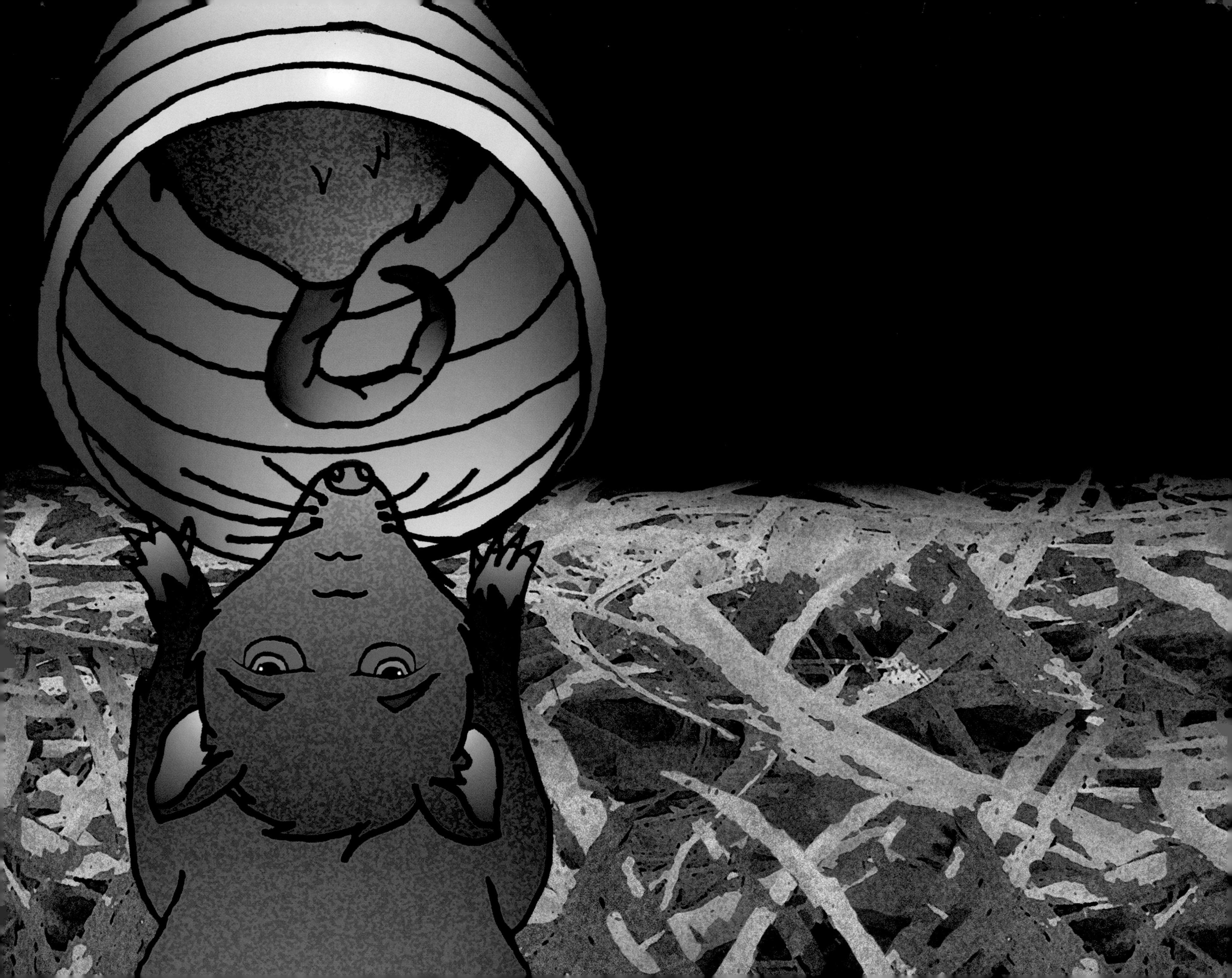

Gray rat shrieks again.
Brown rat shoves him with his nose.
Gray rat moves slowly.

Brown rat keeps pushing
Gray rat until both rats slide
Down the tube. They land.

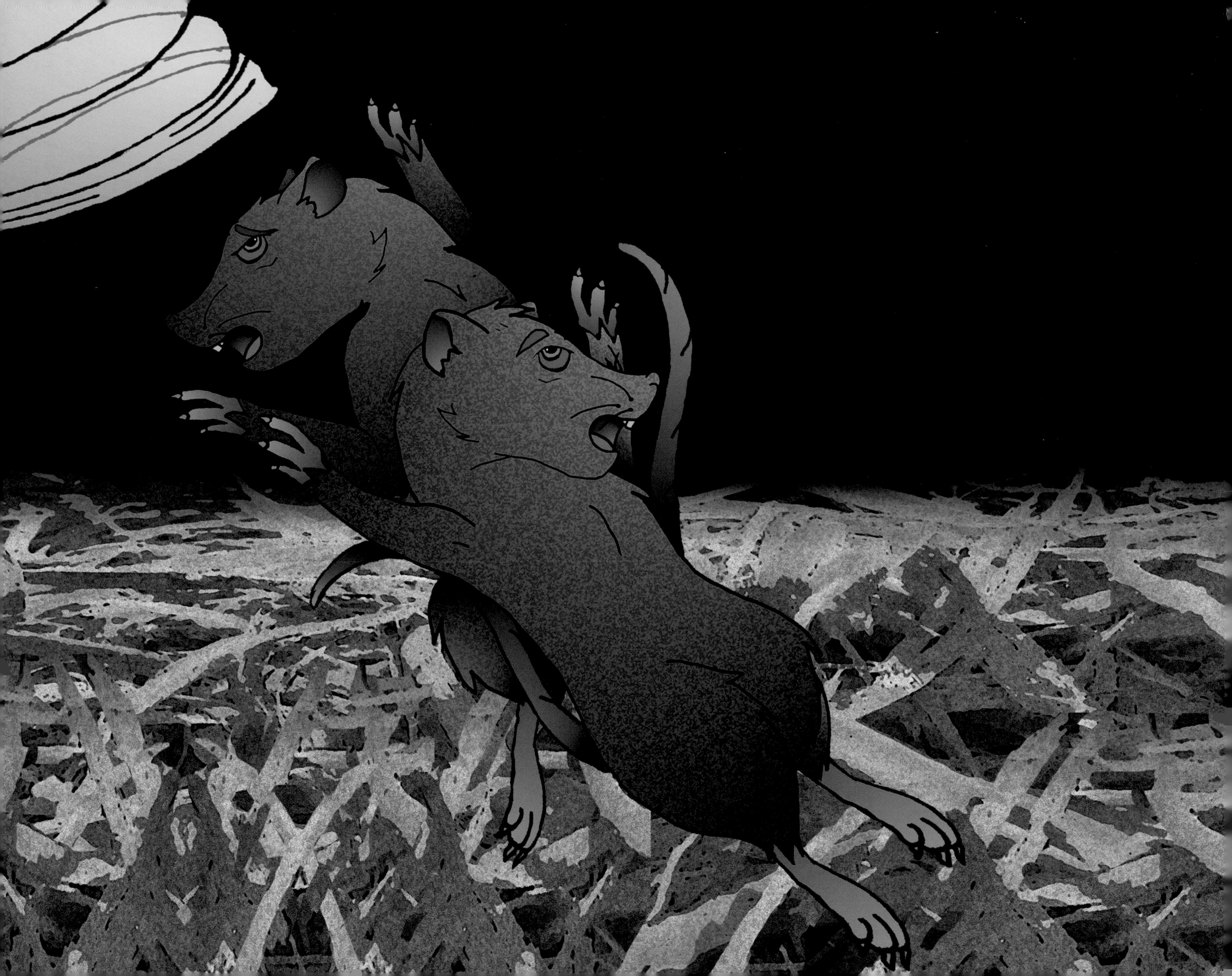

Rats twitch their noses.
That was fun. Let's go again!
They squeeze through tunnel.

Ready! Set! Let's go!
Wheee! Whoosh! *PLOP! PLOP!* They land on
Their fat tails. Again.

This time they go way
Up to the top. One . . . Two . . . Three!
Down they go! *PLOP! PLOP!*

Playing together
Is much more fun than running
And eating alone.

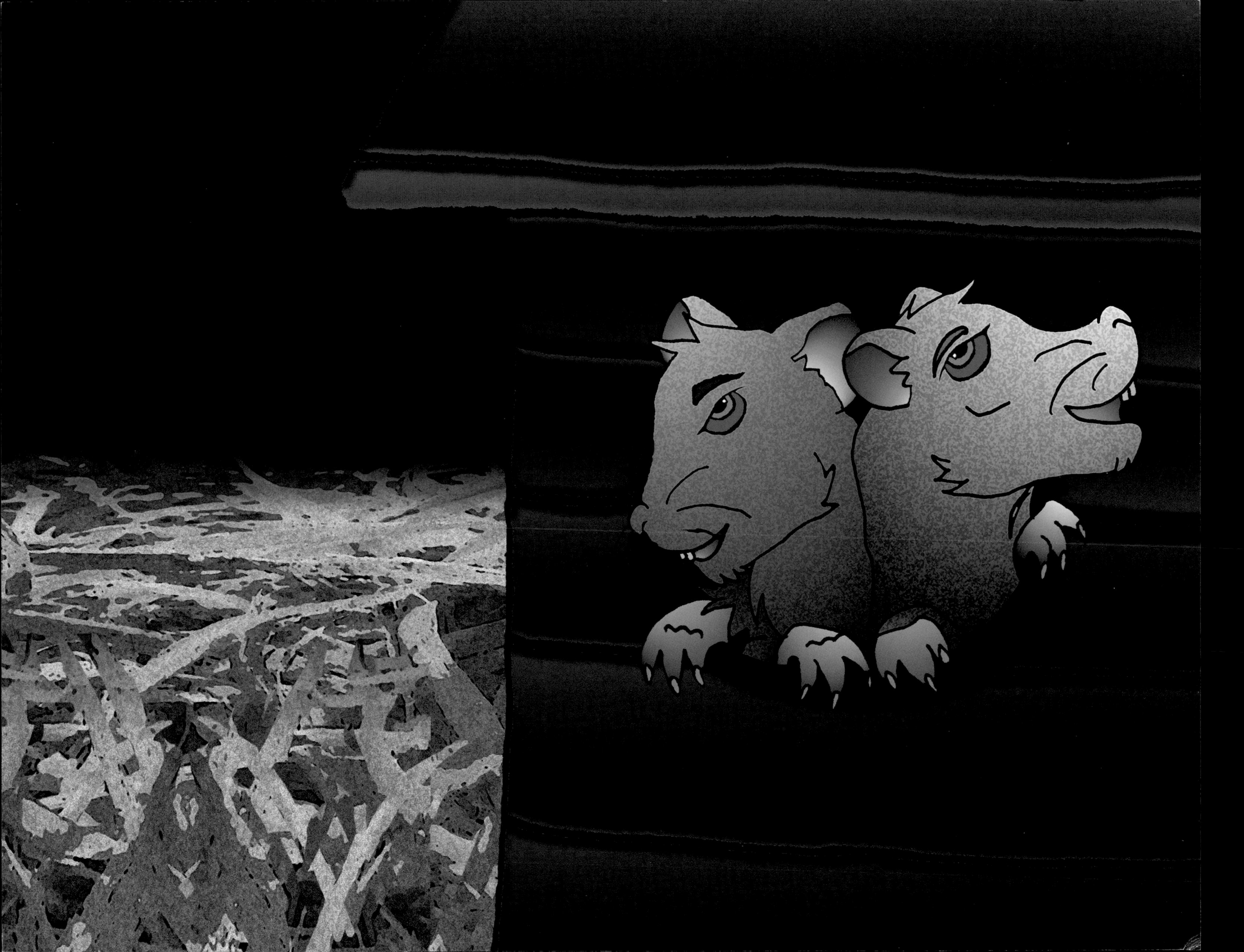

Rat tank is filled with
Shrieks and happy rat noises.
Together rats play.

Evening comes and rats
Go to sleep dreaming of games
For another day.

About the Author

Kristina Henry grew up in Vienna, Virginia. She graduated from Washington College in Chestertown, Maryland. Henry has worked as a technical writer, public relations director and substitute teacher. Her work has appeared in The Washington Post, USA Today, and The Washingtonian magazine. She is the author of the books, *The Fish Tank*, *The Rat Tank,* and *The Turtle Tank,* as well as *Sam: The Tale Of A Chesapeake Bay Rockfish.* She lives in Easton, Maryland, with her husband Mike.

About the Illustrators

Laura Ambler is proof that you don't need to leave home to reinvent yourself. The former Telly Award-winning advertising executive was bored in her industry and looking for something new to stir her creative juices. In Insert image 1998 she enrolled in a screenwriting class offered at Johns Hopkins University and a year later had launched a career in Hollywood—without ever leaving her hometown of Easton, Maryland.

Ambler is a member of the Writer's Guild of America East and has written approximately twenty screenplays, including *The White Pony*, produced by legendary producer and director, Roger Corman. She also wrote and produced the children's videos *Horses A to Z*, *Airplanes A to Z*, and *I Love Horses*.

Amanda Brown was born and raised on the Eastern Shore of Maryland. Her illustrations have appeared in *The Fish Tank*, *The Turtle Tank*, and *The Rat Tank*. She currently lives with two crazy kittens, Zero and Yukki, in Easton, Maryland, where she attends a local college. In her spare time, Amanda enjoys cooking, sewing, and drawing comics about her friends.